You Are Invited
to
Yonderfel's
Castle
All Are Welcome
No exceptions.
No kidding.

Yonderfel's Castle

by Jean Gralley

Henry Holt and Company & New York

For Nancy Wilson

Henry Holt and Company, LLC
Publishers since 1866
175 Fifth Avenue
New York, New York 10010
www.HenryHoltKids.com

Henry Holt® is a registered trademark of Henry Holt and Company, LLC.

Distributed in Canada by H. B. Fenn and Company Ltd.

Library of Congress Cataloging-in-Publication Data
Gralley, Jean.
Yonderfel's castle / by Jean Gralley. — 1st ed.
p. cm.
Summary: King Yonderfel, once renowned and beloved for his generous hospitality, has been lonely since an ogre caused all of his guests to leave, but when a flood brings them all paddling back, the king happily goes back to turning no one away.
ISBN-13: 978-0-8050-6329-5 / ISBN-10: 0-8050-6329-3
[1. Fairy tales. 2. Kings, queens, rulers, etc.—Fiction. 3. Castles—Fiction. 4. Hospitality—Fiction. 5. Ghouls and ogres—Fiction.] I. Title.
PZ8.G74638Yon 2008 [E]—dc22 2008038227

First Edition—2009 / Designed by Véronique Lefèvre Sweet
Printed in March 2009 in China by South China Printing Company Limited, Dongguan City, Guangdong Province, on acid-free paper. ∞

10 9 8 7 6 5 4 3 2 1

Long ago and high, high in the air, there was once a most terrific castle. King Yonderfel ruled the castle and he ruled it splendidly. All day long he stood at the gate, calling "Come in, come in!" to all who passed by, and he never ever turned anyone away.

Naturally, his castle was
a crowded and happy place.

Dancers came and singers came and eaters and kissers came, so there was dancing and singing and eating and kissing . . .

and for years everyone had magnificent times.

One day . . .

. . . an ogre guy came to the back door with a paper. It said he was doubling the rent on the mountain. (He owned the mountain and could do that, even to a king.)

"Oh dear," said the king. "I let my people stay here for free. I can only give you *half* what you ask!"

"Then I shall take away *half* the mountain," said Ogre Guy.

"Outrageous!" cried the king.

"Tough petunias," sniffed the ogre, and with a shrug he sank a gigantic hook into the mountainside and started up his tractor.

WHOA!

Alas, poor Yonderfel! He tried to make the best of things.

But travelers went around him,

and children made fun of him,

and townspeople came with a petition, declaring King Yonderfel clearly a cabbage-headed nincombooby and his castle a hazard to the community.

KNIT 1 PURL 2 KNIT 1 PURL 2

. . . and long, long years.

One day, in the valley where everyone had forgotten there ever was a king, the sky changed. It began to rain.

It started like ordinary rain . . .

. . . but it wasn't. It rained till rain came up to windowsills and into windows, till rooms filled and tables floated and no one could touch bottom.

Just as water rose over noses and ears, someone remembered the king with the castle high in the air and how, best of all, he never turned anyone away.

Everyone paddled for Yonderfel's castle.

Seeing them coming, Yonderfel leaped for joy. He grabbed his towels and ran to the gate, calling "Come in! Come in!"

Each and every person was dried and sent to the fireplace to be warmed. Before long everybody was eating and dancing and singing and having a most magnificent time.

But the more people Yonderfel pulled into the castle, the farther the castle leaned over the cliff. It teetered. It tottered. Then it tippy-tip-tipped! Everyone gasped.

In the quiet, a little voice outside cried, "Let me in! Take me in, please!"

It was Ogre Guy!

People cried, "Alas! Alack! If one more comes in, the castle will fall!"

"Close the gates and close them NOW!"

For the first time ever, Yonderfel wasn't sure what a good king should do.

Finally, he did what he'd always done before: he stretched out his hand and . . .

WOE is US!
This is what comes of
HAVING A CABBAGE-HEADED~
ADDLE-BRAINED~
FOOZLE-NOODLED~
NINCOMBOOBY FOR A KING!!!
uh-oh.

And so . . .

. . . it *seemed* like the end.

But it wasn't.

With huge guest towels billowing, Yonderfel's castle rose above the waves. It glided gracefully like a ship of a hundred sails, full and bright as a golden heart.

The castle settled on a new mountaintop where conditions were about perfect for living happily ever after. And once the sun came out again . . .

. . . that's just what happened.

After many years the good king died. But his castle continued to have magnificent times because Yonderfel's people took turns standing at the gate, calling "Come in! Come in!" to all who passed by. And they never ever turned anyone away.